Dear Barbie™

Riding Champion

By L. L. Hitchcock
Illustrated by S. I. Artists

A GOLDEN BOOK • NEW YORK

Golden Books Publishing Company, Inc., Racine, Wisconsin 53404

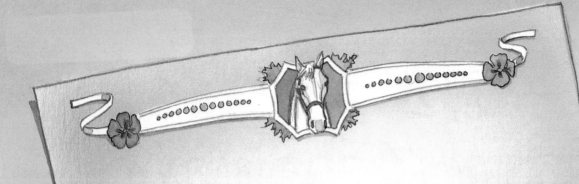

Dear Barbie,

I wish I had a horse! It would be really fun to learn how to ride. I dream about being in a horse show someday.

I know you have a horse named Rosebud. Have you ever been in a show?

Love,
Emma

Barbie sat down to answer Emma's letter. *"Dear Emma,"* she wrote. *"Rosebud and I have been in many horse shows. Let me tell you about an exciting adventure we had last summer. My sister Skipper was competing for the first time at the State Fair show."*

Barbie continued her letter. This is the story she told . . .

It was a beautiful June day and the big horse show was about to start. Barbie brushed Rosebud until the horse's coat gleamed. "We've worked hard for this, Rosebud," Barbie said. "And we can win. We just have to remember everything we've learned!"

The loudspeaker boomed: "First contestant, please."
Sitting high on Rosebud's back, Barbie touched her heels
to the horse's sides and they entered the ring.
Skipper stood outside, watching. "Good luck!" she called.

When the judge called, "Trot, please," Rosebud made her way around the ring. The judge called out many different orders. Barbie and Rosebud performed everything perfectly.

The next contestant in line was a girl named Linda.

After Linda and the other expert riders had their turns, the judge announced the winner. Barbie had a perfect score—but so did Linda. It was a tie!

"Congratulations!" the judge said. "A blue ribbon and a silver cup for each of you!"

"Wow!" Skipper said to Barbie. "I wish I could ride like you!"
"Someday you will," Barbie said. "Just keep practicing."
Later the loudspeaker crackled: "Novice class is next."
"That's me!" Skipper exclaimed. "Wish me luck!"

Skipper and her horse Daisy entered the ring and waited for the judge's orders.

"If we try really hard, maybe we'll win a prize!" Skipper whispered to Daisy.

Daisy pranced, tossing her head up and down, excited by all
the people and horses.

"Whoa!" said Skipper, pulling in Daisy's reins.

Daisy neighed nervously. The more Skipper tried to pull her
in, the more distressed the horse became.

Suddenly a ray of sunlight flashed off the silver cup—shining straight into Daisy's eyes!

Daisy pulled her head away sharply, yanking the reins from Skipper's grip. Then, without warning, the horse jumped over the gate and out of the ring!

"Oh, no!" cried Barbie.

Barbie leaped onto Rosebud's back and raced after Skipper. "Faster!" Barbie cried, urging Rosebud on. "We must catch them!"

Barbie guided her horse over a stone wall with ease.
"I'm so glad Rosebud trusts me," Barbie thought. "We make
a great team!"

Barbie and Rosebud raced into the woods.

"Uh-oh!" Barbie cried when she spotted a stream ahead. "It's okay, Rosebud," she urged in a reassuring tone. "We're fine."

Without stopping, Rosebud splashed through!

Suddenly they came out of the woods to a clearing. Barbie cried, "Oh, no! There's a high fence up ahead! I've got to stop them before Daisy tries to jump it!"

"Come on, girl," Barbie said to Rosebud. "We're almost there."
Barbie reached out for Daisy's reins—but she missed! Quickly
Barbie tried again. This time she caught the reins.

Barbie pulled Daisy to a stop. "Are you all right?" Barbie asked anxiously as she helped Skipper dismount.

Skipper nodded. "Wow! What went wrong?" she asked.

"Horses get scared, just like people," Barbie said. "But they can't talk about their fears. All Daisy could do was run."

Once Barbie was sure that Skipper and Daisy were calm, she gave her sister a leg-up onto the horse.

"Look," Skipper said. "Linda and the judge are coming."

"Thank goodness you're safe!" the judge called to Skipper. Then he turned to Barbie. "You really rode like a champion!"

Linda agreed with the judge. "I'm so proud to share first place with you," she told Barbie.

Barbie smiled as she finished her letter to Emma.

"... *You see,*" Barbie wrote, "*it takes time and hard work for a rider and horse to become a team. But it's worth the effort! Skipper found that out. She and Daisy are winning ribbons now!*

"*I've enclosed a special photo for you. I hope that someday you will have a chance to try for a blue ribbon, too!*

Love,
Barbie

It is Sid.

2

Sid can dip in it.
What is it?

Sid can dig for it.
What is it?

3

4

Sid can fill it.
What is it?

Sid can fix it.
What is it?

5

6

Sid can sit in it.
What is it?

Sid can hit it.
What is it?

7

8

Sid can win it.
What is it?

JUST FOR FUN

Ask someone to help you read and do these activities.

Rhyming Words

1. Think of five words that rhyme with **hit**.

2. Ask someone to help you write the five words on a piece of paper.

Sid Can Do It

1. Tell someone about your favorite thing that Sid can do.

2. Draw a picture of something else you think Sid can do. Ask someone to help you write a sentence about your picture.

PHONICS READERS
STECK VAUGHN

What Is It?

Phonetically Sequenced Stories in This Set

STECK-VAUGHN
C O M P A N Y

ISBN 0-8114-5152-6

90000

9 780811 451529

Space Fox
and Wild Bird

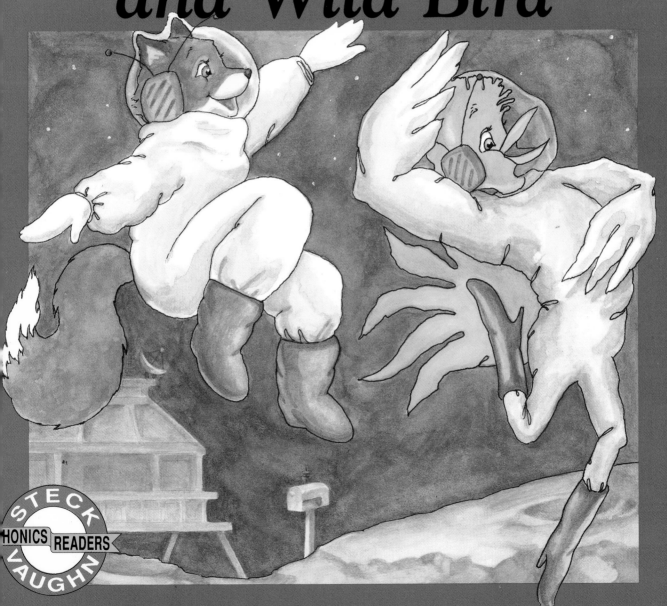

Set 3–Blends
Book 9–Final Blends

Space Fox and Wild Bird

Story by Alice K. Kunka
Illustrations by Rhonda Childress

Staff Credits

Executive Editor: Elizabeth Strauss
Project Editor: Susan A. Miller
Design Manager: Cynthia Ellis

ISBN 0-8114-5180-1

STECK-VAUGHN
C O M P A N Y
A Subsidiary of National Education Corporation